TWICE TEMPTED

ELIZABETH KELLY

EK PUBLISHING INC.

TWICE TEMPTED

Would you risk it all for love?

Lucy Reid was attracted to her sexy new boss, Jason Young, from the first day she met him. After being trapped in an elevator together reveals his secret attraction to her, they embark on a sizzling week-long affair.

Lucy is adamant about keeping their relationship a secret from their coworkers. But when Jason wants more, she must decide if dating her boss is worth risking her job and her reputation.

CHAPTER 1

Lucy rang the doorbell of the large two-story house. She'd hemmed and hawed over going for most of the afternoon, and still wasn't sure that she'd made the right decision. The door opened, Jerry's wife Heather beamed at her in delight, and she was suddenly glad she came.

"Lucy! Honey, it's so good to see you. I keep telling Jerry to invite you over for dinner, but you know him. He just grumbles about keeping his professional life separate and sneaks off to his shop in the back to tinker with his cars. Which is silly because the man loves you like you're one of his own daughters."

Lucy flushed a little and Heather laughed. "It's true. I know he acts all gruff and serious at the office but he's such a softie. Oh, he'd kill me if he knew I was telling you this." She looked around before leaning forward and whispering conspiratorially, "You've always been his favourite at the office."

Lucy laughed. "Well don't you tell him this, but he's always been my favourite as well."

Heather looked her up and down. "You look lovely tonight."

"Thank you," Lucy said. "I wasn't sure if this was a formal or casual event, so I threw a skirt on rather than my jeans just in case."

"You would have looked just as lovely in jeans, my dear. Besides, it doesn't matter what you're wearing – we have a mixture of everything tonight."

"It was really nice of Jerry to do this," Lucy said.

"I thought so too. Jerry thought it would be good to have a bit of a shindig for everyone at the office. You've all been working so hard for the last six months, and the company has been doing so well that you deserve a night of celebration."

Lucy was still standing on the doorstep and Heather smacked herself in the head. "Oh, for heaven's sake! Come in – come in! I didn't mean to leave you standing on the doorstep like a lost waif."

"The others are gathered in the living room and the dining room. Go start mingling and I'll grab you a glass of wine," Heather said.

Lucy went down the hallway and into the living room. She scanned the room. Nearly everyone from the office was there, and the living room and adjoining dining room were filled with people. Alex was standing by the fireplace talking with Maureen and Wallace. Jerry was standing next to Carol and gesturing wildly, his face already a bit red from the wine.

She scanned the room again, refusing to admit to herself who it was she was looking for. When she didn't see him, her pulse, which was thudding loudly in her ears, quieted down. Ignoring her disappointment, she headed toward Penny who was standing next to the large bay window.

"OH MY GOD! LOOK WHO JUST WALKED THROUGH THE door." Penny couldn't hide the glee from her voice. It was just over an hour later. Lucy was telling Penny about the time her cousin had tried to stuff her into the dryer, when Penny had interrupted her with a soft squeal.

Lucy glanced behind her. Jason had walked into the living room. Immediately her face flushed, and her heart galloped into a stroke level rhythm. She turned away swiftly.

"Damn, he looks good," Penny said. "I wonder where he's been for the last two weeks."

Lucy shrugged. "I don't know, and I don't care."

That was a bold-faced lie. Two weeks ago, she'd been in Jason's bed having the best sex of her life and not caring that he was her boss. But she thought grimly, a lot could change in two weeks. The Monday after the weekend she spent with Jason, she was on cloud nine but that changed quickly. By Tuesday he was gone from the office and no one knew why. Not even Carol knew, and she could always be counted on to know exactly where anyone was at any given moment. Lucy had overheard her and Maureen talking in the lunchroom one day and Carol had shrugged when Maureen had asked her about it.

"I don't know. All I know is he had to leave to attend a personal matter." Carol bit into her apple. "Jerry's been taking all his calls and I don't even know when he'll be back."

For the first few days Lucy checked her cell phone constantly, positive that Jason would text her. How many messages had she typed out to him by text, only to delete them without sending? Too many. She wanted to text him, told herself to text him just a casual low-vibe note, but something held her back. As the days turned into a week, her worry turned to anger. He'd been so sweet to her at the beach

3

house that weekend. He had made it sound like he wanted something more than sex. But a man who couldn't be bothered to send a single text in two weeks was sending a clear message, one she hated to receive but ultimately wasn't that surprised by.

Lucy stared into her wine glass. From the day he started, Jason was cold and rude to her. She was positive that he hated her, and she hadn't been that fond of him.

Liar!

Yeah, okay, she was a liar. She'd been attracted to him from the start. The night they were trapped in the elevator together, Jason had finally admitted his rude behavior was an attempt to hide his attraction to her. Giving in to their mutual attraction and having mind-blowing sex on the floor of the elevator was a stupid idea but, even now, one she couldn't regret. Even if fucking your boss multiple times was the ultimate career-ending move.

But two weeks without seeing him, without hearing his deep voice or having him touch her in the way she had grown accustomed to in way too short of a time, had left her feeling lonely and blue. She was confused by her reaction. A weekend of sex did not make a relationship, and she wasn't the type of girl to fall quickly for someone. In fact, she hadn't had a serious relationship in three years, and she was perfectly content with that.

Although Jason had mentioned he wanted it to be more than sex between them, they weren't actually dating yet and he was under no obligation to share anything with her. Still, she couldn't shake her hurt over his two weeks of silence.

He probably regretted what he said. He probably changed his mind about having a relationship with you and used his two weeks away from the office as the perfect way to send a message to you. You're stupid if you think he would risk his entire career just to spend some time between your legs. You're good in bed, girl, but you're not that good.

Lucy took a large gulp of wine. That was another thing – despite her poofy hair, extra few pounds, and pale-as-a-freaking-vampire skin – she'd always had loads of self-confidence. She'd never doubted her ability to get or keep a man until Jason Young came along, and she hated that he rattled her confidence so much.

So what if he didn't want her? Like her mom always said - there were plenty of other fish in the sea. And not one of those fish was her boss. She was better off not having anything to do with Jason Young.

"Lucy? Are you okay?" Penny was staring at her and Lucy forced herself to smile at her.

"Fine. Why?"

"You looked weird for a minute there."

"I'm good."

"Okay, well if you'll excuse me, I think I'll say hello to Jason."

Lucy rolled her eyes. "Seriously, Penny?"

Penny wiggled her eyebrows at her. "Hey, I have an office bet to win, remember? Alex is already glued to his side, and Maureen and June are eyeing him up from across the room."

Lucy walked to the dining room as Penny practically sprinted across the living room to Jason. She stared out the patio doors into the backyard and reminded herself repeatedly not to turn around and stare at Jason.

"Hello, Lucy."

She smiled at the website developer standing next to her. "Hey, Carlos. How are you?"

"I'm good. How are you?"

"I'm well, thanks. Enjoying the party?" Lucy asked.

Carlos was a nice guy, and she had a feeling he was interested in her as more than a co-worker, but he wasn't her type. Forgetting that he was four inches shorter than her, he was loud and boisterous and commanded the attention of the room. She was attracted to the type of guy who radiated a quiet confidence and didn't need to use loud words and grand gestures to get people's attention.

Jason's type.

She groaned to herself. Would she have even one day where she wasn't thinking about her stupidly hot boss?

"I am. It was nice of Jerry to throw this for us." Carlos moved a little closer and squeezed her arm. "Have you gotten something to eat yet?"

"No, I was chatting with Penny and haven't hit the buffet table yet." She looked behind her at the dining room table that was laden with food.

Carlos tugged on her arm and she allowed him to lead her to the table. "Let's grab a bite to eat then."

———

JASON LOOKED OVER ALEX'S SHOULDER, TAMPING DOWN HIS irritation when he watched Carlos squeeze Lucy's arm. He led her to the table, and they helped themselves to the food. Carlos said something to Lucy that made her laugh and Jason frowned. The shorter man was standing way too close to her with his arm brushing against hers. When he led her out of the dining room and into the backyard, Jason had to stop himself from following.

"Jason?" Alex brushed her hand across his chest. "Earth to Jason?"

"Sorry? What?" he said a bit impatiently.

"I asked where you've been for the last two weeks." The blonde woman smiled at him as Penny and Maureen stared at him expectantly.

"It was a personal matter," he said.

"Oh, of course. I'm sorry. I didn't mean to pry," Alex said.

He peered over her shoulder again, but Carlos and Lucy had moved away from the patio door. He bit back his irritation and ignored his urge to find Lucy, throw her over his shoulder and leave the party.

———

LUCY GAVE CARLOS A STIFF SMILE AND MOVED HIS HAND OFF her knee. She'd been trapped in a lawn chair listening to him yammer on and on about himself for nearly two hours now. She had the beginning of a headache, the approaching storm was making the air hot and muggy, and she really had to pee.

Carlos was still a nice guy but if she had to move his hand off her leg once more or listen to him talk about his Star Wars collection for much longer, she was going to lose it. Her gaze flickered to where Jason was standing on the far side of the lawn. He was surrounded by most of the single women in the office, not to mention a few of the married ones, and as usual he looked calm and collected.

He hadn't approached her or even looked at her once since he had arrived at the party, and she was growing angrier by the minute. He was a jerk, she decided. He sweet talked his way between her legs and once he had what he wanted, he dropped her like a hot potato. She watched as Alex rubbed his arm with her hand and Jason smiled down at her. Despite what he had told her, he would move on to Alex next. Lucy was sure of it.

Alex and Maureen left the group of women surrounding Jason and headed for the patio. As they passed her, Alex gave her a large, false smile. Lucy looked away. She'd never gotten along with Alex, even before Jason joined the company, but now most of her annoyance with Alex was wrapped up in the way Lucy felt when Alex flirted with Jason.

She rubbed her forehead and when Carlos's hand crept down to her leg again, she stood up abruptly, nearly knocking her lawn chair over.

"Lucy? What's wrong?" Carlos said.

"Nothing. I need to use the ladies room. Excuse me, please." She turned and walked back to the house. It was blessedly cool inside, and she headed out of the dining room and down the hall toward the bathroom. The door was shut, and she sighed with frustration and leaned against the wall.

The doorway to the kitchen was a few feet away and she could hear Alex and Maureen's voices in the kitchen. When she heard Jason's name, she stepped toward the doorway, leaned against the wall beside it, and shamelessly eavesdropped.

"I swear I'll be taking Jasonhome tonight," Alex said. "Do you see the way he's looking at me?"

Maureen snorted. "I'm not seeing anything but politeness. In fact, he's never anything more than polite to all of us. Well, except for Lucy of course. God, he hates her. I don't know how she comes to work every day. If my boss was that cold and rude, I'd find a new job."

"I'm just hoping that he finally fires her this week. I have Thursday in the betting pool for when he's going to kick her fat ass out of the office," Alex said.

"Speaking of Lucy – did you see Carlos hitting on her?" Maureen asked.

Alex laughed. "I did. What a joke. I have no idea what he sees in her. She's about a foot taller than him and outweighs him by, like, sixty pounds. She'd squish him like a bug the first time they had sex with her fat ass on top. Could you picture the two of them going at it? It gives me the -"

Lucy stepped into the kitchen, smiling when Alex's face turned bright red.

"Hey, Luce." Embarrassment coloured Maureen's voice.

"Hello, Maureen. Hello, Alex. Enjoying the party?" Lucy replied.

"Um, yes, and you?" Maureen said.

"Sure am." She smiled and turned to leave before pausing and looking over her shoulder at the two women. "Oh, and by the way? The men *love* my fat ass. It gives them something to hold on to when things get a little rough in bed."

She wiggled her butt at the two women before sauntering down the hallway. Despite her bad mood, she couldn't help but giggle. She'd been insulted by women like Alex her entire life. But she was fortunate to be blessed with a mother who helped her to understand at an early age that it was their own body insecurities that made them so nasty.

She giggled again and mumbled, "Squish him like a bug. Even if that were true, Carlos would die a happy man."

She was headed away from the bathroom and her bladder suddenly and vehemently reminded her of her need to pee. The door to the bathroom was still closed and she leaned against the wall and waited, jiggling her leg impatiently.

Heather came around the corner from the living room. "Lucy, run upstairs and use the bathroom off our bedroom."

"Oh no, it's fine," Lucy said.

"Don't be silly. Go on now. It's the third door on the left."

9

Heather made a shooing gesture with her hand, and Lucy nodded gratefully before heading up the stairs.

She walked through their large bedroom, it was decorated in shades of gray and cream and really quite stunning, and into the bathroom. Even needing to pee as badly as she did, she still had time to be impressed by the marble counter tops and high-end fixtures. She used the bathroom and was washing her hands when there was a knock on the door.

"Just a minute." She dried her hands and then pulled a hair elastic from her purse and quickly gathered her hair into a messy bun on the top of her head. When she had left for the party it was somewhat straight, but the humidity in the air had brought out her natural wave and now it just looked poofy.

She hesitated and looked at her shirt in the mirror. Although it was snug and highlighted her breasts nicely, she had, as usual, buttoned it nearly to her throat. She unbuttoned the top three buttons and then the fourth. She was wearing a push-up bra and her ample cleavage pushed at the opening of her shirt.

She studied her reflection for a moment. She was tempted to leave her shirt unbuttoned and go back to the party. Alex had nothing on her in the chest department and it wouldn't be the first time Lucy had used her rack to grab a man's attention.

"If you've got it, flaunt it – right?" she muttered. She doubted Jason would be able to ignore her if she left her shirt the way it was. She might not know much about her boss, but she did know the man loved him some boobs. She grinned a little. Alex would be no match for her, and she suddenly wanted to see the look on Alex's face when Lucy came saun-tering outside with her cleavage on display. She'd have a –

Lucy rolled her eyes and brought herself back to reality. She had always prided herself on being completely professional both at work and work functions, and now she was considering throwing that all away because she was jealous. Ridiculous. She was losing it.

She would say goodbye to Heather and Jerry and leave. She'd had about all she could take of Jason ignoring her. As she reached for the buttons on her shirt there was another knock and the door opened.

"Hey, this room is occupied. Oh... hey."

She clasped her hands together in front of her as Jason stepped into the bathroom and closed the door. He leaned against it and stared at her. She swallowed and took a step back. He was dressed in jeans and a tight gray t-shirt that emphasized his broad chest and narrow waist. Her eyes wandered back to his face and she frowned a little. He was as handsome as ever, but now that she was so close to him, she could see the exhaustion on his face and the dark circles under his eyes.

"Hello, little Lucy," he said.

"Hello, Mr. Young."

He frowned. "We're back to formalities?"

"Yes, we are."

"Very well. How have you been, Ms. Reid?"

"Just fine." She cleared her throat. He took a couple of steps forward and she took another step back. His gaze dropped to her chest, and her nipples hardened in response to the look of dark desire in his eyes.

"I like your shirt," he said.

"Thank you. Excuse me, please."

She had to get away from him. Just being this close to him was bringing back all sorts of delicious memories. It didn't help that he was looking at her like he wanted to lick her all over.

She went to step past him, and he grasped her upper arm,

pulling her to a stop. "Are you going back to the party with your shirt like that?"

She looked down at her cleavage. "What's wrong with my shirt? You said you liked it."

"I do," he admitted, "and I have a feeling that Carlos will like it too. Especially since your cleavage is at eye level for him."

She could feel a smile starting and tamped it down. She would not be sucked in by his charm again.

He stepped even closer, his thumb rubbing small circles on the exposed flesh of her arm. "I don't like the way he looks at you." His eyes darkened again but this time with anger. "Or the way he touches you."

She shrugged. "Carlos is a nice guy."

"How nice?" he demanded.

She scowled at him. "That's none of your business, Mr. Young."

He backed her up until she was pressed against the small linen closet door that was opposite of the sink. "I leave for two weeks and suddenly you're sleeping with Carlos? You didn't strike me as that type of girl."

"And what type of girl is that?" She was suddenly furious with him. "I'm not sleeping with Carlos, but what if I did? One – how is that any of your business and two – there's nothing wrong with a woman knowing what she wants and taking it. It's all fine if you want to sleep with me and then move on to Alex, but if I do the same thing then it makes me a slut? That type of double standard is such horseshit!"

He stared at her in surprise. "I'm not sleeping with Alex."

"Not yet." She glared at him. "But you and I both know she's been throwing herself at you for months. You can't tell me you're not interested in her."

"I'm not interested in her." He searched her face. "Lucy, I don't know what's happening. Before I left, we were – well, I thought we were good. Now I come back to see Carlos with his hands all over you, and you're calling me Mr. Young. I don't get it."

"You don't get it?" She rolled her eyes. "You left for two weeks, Jason. You didn't tell me you were going, you didn't text me, you just disappeared. You know, you didn't have to feed me a bunch of bullshit about dating. You could have been truthful with me and said that all you wanted was sex. I'm a big girl, I can handle it."

"I should have texted you. It was just that -"

"Forget it, Jason. You realized that what happened between us was a mistake and scampered off for two weeks to avoid me. I got the message loud and clear, and I happen to agree with it. It was a mistake." She pushed him away and started for the door of the bathroom.

"My mother was sick." Jason's low voice stopped her in her tracks. "She contracted pneumonia and it nearly killed her. My father called Monday night, and I was on a plane first thing Tuesday morning to my hometown. That's where I've been."

She turned around to face him, feeling sick to her stomach. "I'm so sorry, Jason."

He stared at her, his blue eyes dark with worry. "You're right. I should have called or texted you and I'm sorry I didn't. I was spending most of my time at the hospital. My dad was having a rough time with it and I was -"

She shook her head. "Jason, stop. I'm sorry. I assumed and I'm a horse's ass for it. Besides, we aren't dating, and you weren't obligated to let me know what was happening."

He stared at the floor of the bathroom. She hesitated and

then stepped forward, taking his hands tentatively in her own. "How is your mom doing?"

He cleared his throat. "She's better."

She put her arms around Jason's shoulders and gave him a brief hug. He stood stiffly against her and feeling like a complete moron she stepped back. His hands clenched into fists, and then he wrapped his arms around her waist and pulled her into his embrace. She hugged him and rubbed his back as he buried his face in the curve of her neck.

"I'm so sorry," she repeated.

"Thank you." His reply was muffled against her throat. He lifted his head and stared down at her.

"I just got back into town late this afternoon. I wasn't going to come tonight but I wanted to see you." He stroked her cheek with his thumb. "I missed you."

"I missed you too," she admitted.

"Yeah?"

She smiled a little. "Yeah."

He dipped his head and kissed her. It was just a gentle brush of his mouth against hers, but she immediately flattened her body against him and returned his kiss. His tongue slipped into her mouth and she stroked it with her own as he moaned low in his throat.

He backed her up against the linen closet door and she hooked one leg around his waist, pulling him into her. He unbuttoned her shirt as they kissed hungrily, and then worked his fingers under the cups of her bra and cupped her breasts with his warm hands. He kissed down her throat and she lifted her head to give him better access.

"You're so beautiful, Lucy," he muttered against her collarbone. He nipped it, making her gasp, before running his thumbs over her nipples.

She slipped her hands under his t-shirt and ran them

across his bare back, kneading and rubbing at the hard muscles.

"Take off your shirt," she whispered.

He pulled his t-shirt over his head and dropped it onto the counter. She stared appreciatively at his bare chest. Two weeks of being away from the beach had made his skin a little paler but compared to her he still had a rich glow. She ran her fingers through the hair on his chest, and he inhaled sharply when she traced his abs with her short nails.

She slipped her hand into his jeans, pushing past his boxer briefs with impatience until she could wrap her long fingers around his thick cock. He moaned when she gripped him and moved her hand up and down the shaft.

"Shh." She grinned at him.

He slanted his mouth over hers, thrusting his tongue into her mouth as he gripped her thigh in his hand and moved it higher. He squeezed her breast and then ran his hand over the soft swell of her belly under her shirt before his fingers trailed along the inside of her thigh. She thrust her pelvis against him when he traced the material of her underwear.

She stroked his cock faster in response, and he uttered a low curse of need before sliding his fingers under her panties. His thick fingers found her wet opening almost immediately, and he pushed two of them into her. She rocked her hips against him and squeezed his cock.

"That feels so good, little Lucy," he whispered into her ear. "If you keep doing that, I won't be able to stop myself from fucking you right here."

"I don't want you to stop," she whispered.

She stroked him rapidly, feeling the moisture at the tip of him as he moved his fingers in and out of her. She didn't hear a knock and apparently neither did Jason because when the bathroom door opened and Heather stuck her head in, they both froze like frightened rabbits.

"Lucy, are you…" Heather stared at their entwined bodies, her mouth dropping open and her cheeks going pink. "Oh my goodness. Oh – oh my – I'm so, so sorry."

She swung the door shut and Lucy stared wide-eyed at Jason. "Oh shit."

CHAPTER 2

"Heather! Wait!" Lucy chased down the hallway after Heather. She grabbed the older woman's arm and pulled her into their home office. She slammed the door shut behind her and stared frantically at Heather. "You can't say a word about this to anyone."

"I am so sorry, Lucy. I didn't mean to interrupt you. I was just getting worried. You had been gone so long and I -"

"Seriously, Heather. You can't say anything," Lucy said. She grabbed the older woman's hands. "Please, I am begging you."

"Whew, that Jason is a good-looking guy, isn't he? I mean, I love Jerry, but wow – Jason shirtless is quite the vision. If only I were twenty years younger and single," Heather said dreamily.

"Heather!" Lucy shook her a bit frantically. "Focus! You cannot say anything to anyone about what you saw - especially not to Jerry. Please. Do you understand?"

Heather smiled at her. "Honey, of course I do. And I'm not about to say a word to anyone, especially not my husband. I can't imagine what he'd do to Jason if he found out. I told you – he thinks of you like his daughter and he's rather protective of you. Why, just right now he's out there talking to Carlos about appropriate behaviour with co-workers."

"He's what?"

"Poor Carlos. He looked like a schoolboy being scolded – all for putting his hand on your knee." Heather sat down in one of the large leather chairs in the room. "Could you imagine what Jerry would do to Jason if he knew the two of you were having sex in our bathroom?"

"We were not having sex in your bathroom!"

"Not yet you weren't." Heather grinned. "But you totally were going to. Don't try and deny it."

"Oh God," Lucy groaned. She sank into the chair opposite of Heather and put her head in her hands.

Heather patted her shoulder. "Honey, don't worry about it. I won't say a word. I promise."

"Thank you," Lucy said. "I didn't mean for this to happen. Honestly, I didn't. I have no idea what I'm doing or thinking – this is so incredibly inappropriate. I should not be sleeping with my boss."

"Pfft," Heather scoffed. "If I understood Jerry correctly, technically Jason isn't your direct boss. Besides, you're a grown woman and you can do whatever you want."

"That's what Jason says. And I guess technically he isn't. He can't fire me without Jerry's agreement," Lucy said. "But it's still inappropriate.

"If it bothers you that much – find a new job," Heather said blithely. "Jerry will miss you of course, but no job is worth your happiness."

Lucy shook her head. "It's not, I mean, I don't even know where exactly we're going with this and..."

Heather patted her hand. "Don't worry, honey. It'll work

itself out in the end – it always does." She stood and smoothed her straight, sleek bob. "Now, come downstairs and have some dessert."

"Thank you but I think I'm going to head home." Lucy took a deep breath and followed Heather to the door. "I have a bit of a headache and I think it's best if I call it a night. Will you tell Jerry I said thank you and I'll see him on Monday?"

"Of course, dear. Are you going to say goodbye to Jason?"

Lucy shook her head. "No. It's better if I stay away from him. At least until I figure out what I'm going to do."

"YOU HAVE GOT TO BE KIDDING ME!" LUCY CURSED UNDER her breath as there was a muffled thump and her car pulled to the right. She guided her car to the side of the road and climbed out, slamming the door behind her. She stared at the flat back tire as the wind blew strands of her hair around her face. The sky was dark with clouds pregnant with rain.

"Son of a bitch," she muttered. She popped the trunk and pulled the spare tire out from the bottom of it. She rested it against the side of the car before pulling the jack out. As she jacked up the car, the clouds opened up and poured rain down on her.

She squinted in the dark and the rain as she used the jack to hoist up the car. She was soaked to the skin, and so cold she was shaking as she worked at the lug nuts on the tire. They were tightened almost impossibly tight, and she yanked on the socket wrench grimly. Could her night get any worse?

There was a splash of lights and a truck pulled up behind her. She stood, blinking in the glare of the headlights, and held the socket wrench in a tight grip. She had no idea who was behind the wheel of the truck and she tensed as the driver's door opened.

"Jesus Christ, Lucy! What are you doing?"

She sagged against her car as Jason ran to her.

"Why are you driving a truck?" she said stupidly. "You drive a car to work."

"I have both," he said impatiently. "Come on."

He grabbed her hand and led her to his truck. She clambered into the cab of the truck, and he slammed her door shut before running to the driver's side and climbing in. Thunder crashed and lightning flashed across the sky as he shut his door and stared at her.

"What the hell were you doing out there?" He had to shout to be heard over the rain hitting the roof of the truck. It was falling so hard and so fast that she could see nothing out the windshield of the truck except a sheet of water.

She shivered and clasped her cold hands between her knees. Water was dripping off the end of her nose and the lobes of her ears. Her bun had fallen, and she had an idea that her hair was plastered unflatteringly to her head. Her teeth were chattering, and she rubbed her upper arms.

"Christ," Jason swore again and started the truck, turning the heat on high before rummaging in his gym bag in the back seat. He pulled out a towel and slid across the seat.

He unbuttoned her shirt as she shivered. "What the hell were you doing out there, Luce?"

"I had a flat tire." She helped him strip off her wet shirt and didn't object when he wiped her upper body with the towel.

"Why didn't you call me?" He scowled at her.

"I know how to change a tire. My dad taught me when I was sixteen." She returned his scowl before tugging the towel from his hands. She dropped it on the seat between them and pulled her hair elastic from her hair. She towel-dried her hair as Jason angled the heat vents toward her.

"You still should have called me. It's not safe for you to be out here by yourself," he said.

"Please." She rolled her eyes. "I passed a house not two minutes back. I was perfectly safe."

"Next time, you call me. Do you understand?" he demanded. He stripped off his own wet shirt and threw it in the backseat.

"Yes, sir," she muttered.

Her eyes flickered over his naked chest. Lord, he looked good wet. Drops of water clung to the hair on his chest and slid down his ribcage in tiny rivulets. Despite her misery, despite being soaking wet and freezing cold, she wanted to slide across the seat and lick the water from his skin.

"Stop looking at me like that, Lucy," Jason warned in a soft voice she could barely hear over the rain.

She dragged her gaze back to his face. At the look in his eyes, her nipples, already tight with the cold, hardened until they were almost painful and began to throb.

"God, Luce. Do you have any idea what you do to me?" He groaned and slid across the seat. He wrapped her wet hair in his fist, yanked her head back and kissed her hard on the mouth, plunging his tongue between her lips so he could taste her.

They kissed and kissed again, tasting and licking and sucking frantically at each other's tongues as the truck shook with a loud boom of thunder. Jason unhooked her bra and pulled it from her body.

"So pretty," he murmured. He tugged on her arms and she shifted until she was straddling his lap. He cupped her breasts and dipped his head, wrapping his lips around one stiff nipple and teasing it with his warm tongue.

She moaned and clutched at his head. What they were doing was wrong, she knew it was wrong, but she couldn't stop herself. At some point in the last three weeks, she'd become addicted to Jason's touch, and she would do anything to get it.

He laved at her nipples until she was gasping and writhing against him. Each pull of his mouth was a tantalizing combination of pain and pleasure as he used his teeth to scrape across her sensitive nipples. She rocked her pelvis against his rock-hard erection, and he reached under her skirt, growling with frustration at the feel of her panties. They were soaking wet, both from the rain and from her juices, and she gave a soft squeak of surprise when he yanked hard and ripped them off her body.

He dropped them to the floor of his truck and reached between her legs. He ran his fingers over her hard and swollen clit, and she moaned and arched her hips against him. He stroked her repeatedly until the wave of pleasure was cresting in her body. Before it could overtake her completely, he moved his fingers away.

"Why did you leave without saying goodbye to me tonight?" he said.

"What?" Her eyes popped open. "Do you really want to talk about this right now?"

"Yes." He bent his head and licked between her breasts. "Tell me."

"Jason, I don't – I mean, for God's sake, we had just been caught by Jerry's wife. I panicked okay? I talked with Heather, made her promise not to tell anyone, and then I booked it out of there."

"Don't leave me like that again. Promise me," he whispered in her ear. A shudder went through her at his words. Why did it sound like he was talking about something else?

He kissed her mouth. "Promise me, Lucy."

"I promise," she said.

He leaned forward so he could lick and nibble at her throat. She cupped the back of his head, holding him against her as he kneaded her ass and kissed her neck with soft, gentle brushes of his mouth.

"Jason," she sighed and reached between them. Her hands fumbled at his belt, undoing it before popping the button of his jeans and raking the zipper down. He lifted his hips so she could drag his jeans and underwear down to his knees. She took his cock in her hand, rubbing her thumb over the drop of precum that had gathered at the top and then licking it from her thumb.

He groaned with pleasure and reached down to snag a condom out of the pocket of his crumpled jeans. She grinned a little as he ripped open the package.

"Do you just carry one in your pocket all the time now?"

"Only when I know I'm going to see you."

"That's awfully presumptuous of you, Mr. Young." She squeezed his cock, twisting her palm against the shaft in the way she knew he liked.

He held the condom out to her. "Put it on me – now."

The pleasure in her belly pulsed to an almost unbearable level at the tone of his voice. She wouldn't admit it, but she had missed the way he took control in bed and the way he gave her no choice but to obey him. She took the condom from him, glancing up at his face and flushing when she realized she didn't need to admit anything – he could read it on her face.

"Now, Lucy," he prompted, and with a bit of nervous fumbling she smoothed the condom over his large cock.

He bunched her wet skirt up around her waist and rubbed his cock between her legs. She moaned and spread her thighs wide. He guided his cock to her warm and wet opening. He rubbed it down the center of her slit before he arched his hips up, plunging his cock deep inside of her.

She cried out with pleasure as he put one hand on her hip and the other on the back of her neck. Holding her steady, he thrust in and out of her.

"Tell me you want me, Lucy – that you need me."

"I want you. I need you," she moaned.

"Touch yourself," he said.

He took her hand and guided it between her legs. He pressed her fingers against her pussy and she rubbed at her clit. He leaned back and watched, his cock swelling inside of her at the sight of her fingers rubbing herself. He thrust in and out rapidly as she rubbed at her clit.

"Say it again," he demanded.

"I want you, Jason."

"I want you too, little Lucy."

The pleasure was growing in her, circling and twisting in her pelvis and belly, and she rubbed her clit frantically as Jason's hard cock plunged in and out of her. She arched her back, her soft cries turning into loud moans as her orgasm shuddered through her. Vaguely she was aware of Jason gripping her hips, of his own loud moan as he thrust and bucked and came beneath her, and she collapsed against him in a boneless heap.

He panted against her throat, his hard hands rubbing her bare back. "God, I've missed you, little Lucy."

She pushed herself up and smiled down at him. "I missed you too, Jason."

She moved clumsily off his lap, her legs still weak from the strength of her orgasm. She pushed her skirt down, wincing at the cold wetness of the fabric as he slid his pants and underwear back up over his hips. He pulled the condom off, tied it closed, and threw it into an empty grocery bag on the back floor of the truck. He buttoned his jeans as Lucy pulled on her shirt without bothering with her bra. The damn thing was hard enough to put on when it was dry. It would be nearly impossible when it was wet.

"Are you still cold?"

She shook her head no and he turned the heat down before turning on the windshield wipers. The rain had slowed but lightning could still be seen flashing in the sky. He started to pull onto the road and she frowned.

"Jason, wait. I can't leave my car here."

"Yes, you can. I'll come back and change the tire tomorrow."

"I need my purse and my house keys, and I need to lock the car." She reached for the handle of the door, but he had already opened his and was sliding out.

"Stay here. I'll grab them."

He was back in less than two minutes with her purse and keys, and she gave him a smile of thanks before clicking her seat belt into place.

"Show me the way home, little Lucy." He grinned at her.

CHAPTER 3

"This is my apartment building here." Lucy pointed to the tall, grey building on the right. Jason parked on the street in front of the building, and she smiled at him before stuffing her bra into her purse.

"Thank you for the lift home."

"I'll walk you to your door."

"Oh no, you don't have to do that," she said.

"It's not safe for you to be walking alone this late," he said.

She laughed. "Jason, it's only nine and it's less than forty feet to my apartment building. I'll be fine."

"Nope," he said.

He was out of the truck before she could protest again. He opened her door and lifted her out of the truck. It was still raining hard, although not quite the torrential downpour it was earlier. He took her hand and they sprinted to the front door of the apartment building. They stood in the lobby, panting and grinning at each other as water dripped from their bodies.

"Which floor are you on?"

"The second. Thanks again," she said.

"I'll walk you up to your apartment. You never know what kind of riff-raff is hanging around in the stairwell," he said with a grin.

They hiked up the stairs and she led them to her apartment door. She opened it and he stepped inside, staring around curiously at the small and tidy space.

"This is nice."

"Thanks. So, um, I guess I'll see you Monday at the office?" She was suddenly feeling awkward again. Two weeks ago, she had been ready to date him. Convinced that it was perfectly fine to sleep with and date her boss on the sly. But two weeks without him, without hearing his voice or seeing him, had helped bring her back to her senses. What she was doing was madness - an intoxicating and sweet kind of madness - but madness still the same. Her lust for him was satiated earlier in the truck and now her common sense was kicking back in. As much as she wanted him, she couldn't stand the thought of being known as the girl in the office who was sleeping with the boss. They had already been caught by Heather. How much longer until they were caught by her coworkers? By Jerry?

"Actually," he stepped forward and took her hips, pulling her against his growing erection, "I was thinking I would see you in your shower." He nuzzled her throat, his hands massaging her hips through her wet skirt.

"That's not a good idea, Jason," she said as her lust for him came roaring back. "I've been thinking and -"

"You think too much, Lucy." His lips swept up her neck to her ear and nibbled lightly. "Would you like to know what I'm thinking?"

"Yes," she whispered. Her hands locked around his waist.

"I was thinking I'll join you in the shower. I was thinking

I'll use that sweet-smelling soap you own to wash every inch of your delectable body, and then I'll make you suck my cock until I come in your mouth."

She arched her hips against him, pressing herself against his erection, and he chuckled in her ear. "I think you like that idea."

"Jason -"

"Then," he continued as if she hadn't spoken, "I'll take you to your bedroom, lay you down on your bed, spread those long legs of yours and lick your pussy until you come. Then I'll do it again."

"Oh God," she muttered.

His hands slipped under her wet shirt to rub her bare back. "After that, I'm going to put you on your hands and knees and fuck you slowly until you're begging for me to make you come. Would you like that, sweet Lucy?"

"Yes," she moaned.

"Good." He leaned down and dropped a kiss on the tip of her cold nose.

"And in the morning, I'll make you breakfast. I make excellent waffles." He grinned cheerfully at her.

She gaped at him for a moment and then burst into giggles.

"Do you doubt my waffle making skills, Ms. Reid?" he asked.

"No."

"Good. Because they're second only to my ability to make you come, and I think we both know how well I can do that." He kissed her nose again and stared expectantly at her.

She hesitated and then succumbed to the sweet madness. "Actually, Mr. Young. I think I might need a refresher course on that."

A grin lit up his face and she yelped when he bent and

lifted her over his shoulder in a fireman's carry. She found herself face down over his back being smothered by her own breasts.

"I can't breathe!" Her voice was stifled by her chest and she wiggled and squirmed against him.

He slapped her firmly on the ass. "Quiet, woman. I'm in need of servicing – point me to your bedroom."

She pinched him hard on his butt through his wet jeans. He jumped before sliding his hand under her skirt and cupping her between the legs. "The bedroom, woman, before I take you right here in the hallway."

She said something but it was too muffled for him to hear. He shifted her slightly and she lifted her upper body a little as he said, "What was that, Ms. Reid?"

"I said I'm being suffocated by my own boobs. Put me down before I asphyxiate."

He laughed and strode down the hallway. "I guess I'd better find the bedroom quickly then."

———————

LUCY ROSE UP ON HER ELBOWS SO SHE COULD WATCH AS Jason's dark head dipped between her pale thighs once more.

"Oh," she sighed as his tongue pushed inside of her. He was kneeling on the floor beside the bed and her legs were draped over his shoulders. As he replaced his tongue with his fingers and licked a searing path up to her clit, she was helpless to stop her legs from squeezing around his head. He had brought her to an explosive orgasm not five minutes earlier but already she could feel the familiar heat uncurling in her belly. As his tongue darted and flicked and swirled around her clit, she let her head fall back and pumped her hips against his face.

"You're so good at that, Jason. So good," she panted. "Don't stop, please don't stop, don't…"

Another orgasm raced through her and she collapsed against the bed, her limbs sliding off his shoulders. He stood and covered her naked body with his own. He kissed her, pushing his tongue into her mouth until the taste of him on her tongue was replaced by her own.

"On your hands and knees, little Lucy."

He rolled her over and she rose obediently to her hands and knees. He put on a condom and knelt on the bed between her legs. He caressed her ass for long moments, sliding his cock up and down her wet slit until she pushed back against him impatiently.

"Please, Jason." She looked back at him, her eyes dark with a fiery need. "I want you inside of me."

He groaned and thrust into her. He tried to withdraw, and she tightened around him, keeping him inside of her.

"Jesus, Lucy." He gathered her long dark hair into a ponytail and pulled her head back until he could kiss her full mouth. He reached under her and cupped her breast as he rocked inside of her.

He straightened and used his knees to push her pale thighs farther apart. Still holding her hair, he pulled until her back arched and she was staring at the ceiling. He pressed down on the small of her back with his other hand and thrust in and out of her. She squeezed and released him repeatedly with her inner muscles and he panted harshly.

"Please stop doing that, Lucy. You're going to make me come," he suddenly begged.

She grinned saucily. "I like it when you beg, Jason."

He growled, his hand tightening in her hair until she gasped, but she continued to tease him with her muscles as he pushed in and out of her.

"Lucy," he groaned.

He let go of her hair and clamped his hard hands around her hips. He plunged wildly in and out of her before shouting and thrusting so deeply into her that she collapsed under his weight. He pinned her to the bed, his body shaking, as his orgasm rushed through him.

———

JASON ROLLED OFF OF LUCY, DISPOSING OF THE CONDOM IN the garbage beside the bed before turning back to her. She had curled onto her side and when he relaxed next to her, she gave him a warm and lazy smile.

His brushed her hair from her face and kissed her. He realized with a small trickle of fear that he belonged to her now – body and heart and soul. Lucy had started off as a fun distraction for him and now, only a few short weeks later, he couldn't imagine life without her. The thought both frightened and delighted him. He'd been in love only once before, and it had been a slow and almost thoughtful process for him. There was never this moment of clarity, this complete and utter surety that he had found the one for him.

"You're so lovely, Jason," she whispered sleepily.

He snuggled in closer to her as she sighed and closed her eyes.

"Little Lucy?"

"What?" She buried her face into his neck.

"Don't go to sleep. Not yet."

"I'm tired," she pouted.

"I know." He kissed her forehead. "Open your eyes, honey."

"What?" She blinked at him drowsily.

"Tell me about your childhood."

She blinked again. "What do you want to know?"

"Everything."

LUCY DRUMMED HER FINGERS NERVOUSLY ON THE COUNTER AS she listened to the shower shut off. It was late Sunday afternoon and Jason had spent the entire weekend at her apartment. Saturday morning, they had retrieved her car. Jason changed the tire for her and then he made a quick stop at his house to feed Lenny and grab some clothes before returning to her.

The weekend had passed in a blur of sex and sleeping and sharing of stories. Jason was open and warm, telling her everything he could think of about himself. He was a natural storyteller, and she was fascinated by the information he shared. She could hardly believe that she used to think him cold and rude. He was funny and sweet and took great delight in teasing her until she was blushing and flustered. He hadn't just talked about himself. In fact, he was relentless in his need to know everything about her. Lying in her bed, tucked against his warm body with the only light coming from the moon through the window, it was surprisingly easy to tell him things she had never shared with previous boyfriends.

Boyfriend?

Her stomach churned nervously. Is that what he was to her now? She swiped her hand across her forehead. She didn't have a clue what he was. She only knew that at some point in the last day or so, Jason had become more important to her then she could ever have imagined. And that scared the shit out of her. Having a brief, sex-filled fling with her boss was one thing but falling in love with him was an entirely different set of problems.

You're not in love with him. You're not. You're not the type of girl who falls in love with someone after only a few short weeks.

She stared at the closest kitchen chair. Jason had sat on that chair yesterday afternoon and bent her naked body over his lap. He held her firmly with one arm across her back and spanked her again. He had alternated the firm slaps with slow caresses of her ass until she was squirming with desire, her hands squeezing the legs of the chair and her toes curling. She was embarrassed by how much it turned her on.

She could still remember the feel of his erection pushing against her belly, the way he had occasionally dipped his hand between her legs to gauge her wetness, and how at the end she begged him repeatedly to fuck her. He'd lowered her to the floor and taken her, his deep voice whispering a continuous litany of dirty talk and compliments into her ear, until she came screaming beneath him.

She tapped her finger against her lower lip and looked out the doorway into the small living room, trying to calm her aching for him. It was a mistake. She immediately zeroed in on the couch and her blue scarf that still lay across the arm of it. They had ordered pizza Saturday night, sitting side by side and sharing the large pizza as they watched bad reality TV.

After a couple of hours, Jason shut of the TV and disappeared into her bedroom. She was about to follow him when he returned with one of her scarves in his hands. He stared at her with his eyebrows lifted in silent question. When she nodded her consent, he tied her hands behind her back before starting a delicious torment of soft touches and feather-light kisses. He bent her over the back of the couch, spread her legs as she pulled helplessly at the scarf, and brought her to orgasm three times before allowing himself to come.

She turned abruptly and started unloading the dishwasher. If she was completely honest with herself, it wasn't the rough sex or the bondage that was really freaking her out. She could accept that there was a part of her that liked being tied up and enjoyed submitting to Jason in bed. It was the other side of him, the side that had crept in so silently and sneakily that she hadn't even noticed it until this morning, that was making her nervous.

At some point over the weekend, Jason had stopped fucking her and started making love to her. Even when he was rough, even when he was pinning her hands above her head and talking dirty into her ear, there was a tenderness in his touch that wasn't there before.

Not half an hour ago she had been under him, loving the contrast of the soft mattress below her and his hard body above her as he moved in and out of her. He was so sweet, so loving and careful with her that she'd had her strongest orgasm yet. He had made her look at him as he brought her closer and closer to the brink, and she couldn't look away from the warmth radiating from his eyes even when she was coming wildly beneath him.

Good God, what was happening between them?

She wrenched open the silverware drawer and threw the cutlery into it. She jumped when Jason wrapped his arms around her waist and squeezed affectionately.

"What did the spoons do to piss you off?" he asked.

She didn't laugh, and he turned her around. "Hey, what's wrong?"

"What are we doing?"

"What do you mean?"

"I mean this. What's happening between us? What happens tomorrow when we go back to the office?"

"Well, my plan is to do my work and try not to think

35

about how you look bent over my desk with your ass in the air," he teased.

"Jason." She refused to let him lighten the mood.

He sighed and stepped away from her, raking his hand through his hair. "You're thinking too much again, Lucy. Can't we just enjoy our time together and not worry about being caught by our coworkers?"

She shook her head. "I can't do that. What kind of relationship could we possibly have? Always sneaking to each other's places, never being able to go out to a movie or to dinner without worrying that we might run into someone from the office. What kind of relationship is that?"

"We don't have to sneak around. I told you before that there's no firm rule about dating in the office."

"And I told you that I'm not interested in being known as the girl who's banging the boss."

"Is that all this is to you? Just sex?" he asked.

She hesitated, and he swore under his breath.

"Jason, please. You know I can't -"

"I love you, Lucy," he said.

Her mouth fell open and she stared at him in shock. "No, you don't."

"Yes, I do," he said.

"Jason, you're not in love with me. People don't just fall in love after a few weeks. We're great in bed together but that doesn't mean it's love."

"I know. But I am in love with you. I want to be with you, Luce. If that means I have to quit my job, I will." He smiled sweetly at her.

She stared at him in horror. "You cannot quit your job for me."

He laughed and pulled her against him. "I can do whatever I want. You're not the boss of me."

She didn't laugh, and he stroked her cheek. "I love you, Lucy Reid. And I know you love me."

She looked down at his chest and he put his fingers under her chin and tipped her head up. Her dark eyes were swimming with tears.

"I don't love you, Jason," she lied.

The look of hurt on his face nearly destroyed her. He stepped away from her as the hurt was replaced by a look of careful neutrality. "I guess I was mistaken."

"I'm sorry," she said.

"You're sorry?" He laughed bitterly. "Yeah, me too."

She followed him into the bedroom, watching as he packed his bag, but unable to think of a single thing to say. He started to leave the room and she called his name in a strangled voice.

He turned. "Yes?"

She winced at the coldness in his eyes and face. "I really am sorry."

"I'll see you at work tomorrow, Ms. Reid."

He left her bedroom and when she heard the front door of her apartment slam shut, she collapsed on the bed and wept bitterly into her pillow.

CHAPTER 4

"Lucy, will you tell me what's wrong?"

She jumped in her chair and then spun it around. Jerry was standing in her office. He had entered and shut the door without her even hearing him.

Of course she hadn't heard him. It was Friday of the longest week of her life, and she spent each day barely able to concentrate on her work. She had made a mistake. She had known that from the moment Jason left her apartment. On Monday she tried to speak to him, tried to explain that she was scared and confused about her feelings, but he shut her down before she could even begin.

He had looked at her with such anger and with no trace of his former warmth that she'd wilted under his gaze. She whispered once more that she was sorry and escaped his office, barely able to make it to the bathroom before the hot tears fell.

Since then, she tried to avoid him, but it seemed like every time she turned around, she was bumping into him or being forced into some meeting that he was in as well. He either outright ignored her or spoke so rudely and dismissively to her, that her coworkers were beginning to question her about what she'd done.

Penny, in particular, questioned her extensively. Lucy played dumb and did her best to convince Penny that his behaviour wasn't any different than it was before. She even managed to joke about putting in her own guess for the 'when would Jason fire her' bet. Penny wasn't convinced, but she had studied Lucy's pale face and the dark circles under her eyes before changing the subject.

Now, Lucy plastered a smile on her face and stood up. "What do you mean, Jerry?"

"There's obviously something wrong and I want you to tell me what I can do to fix it," he said.

She almost started to cry but blinked the tears back fiercely. What had happened to logical, self-controlled Lucy? The old Lucy would never have cried in front of her boss.

"I'm – I'm not feeling very well this week," she fibbed.

"Does it have something to do with Jason?" he asked.

She paled. "Why would you think that?"

"I'm not blind, Lucy. I've seen how rude he's been to you in the last week. He's being completely unprofessional, and I'm going to speak to him about it."

"No! Please don't do that, Jerry." She swallowed nervously. "I - I've been so preoccupied with this other thing that I've been making mistakes in my work. You've seen it and so has Jason. He's only being rude because he knows I can do better."

"Do you need to take some time off? We can arrange for you to take a few weeks." Jerry patted her arm awkwardly.

"No. I'll be fine." She wanted more than anything to not be at the office but how would that solve the problem? There was only one way to solve this mess and it involved her finding a new job. Her stomach dropped at the thought of leaving the office and the work that she loved.

As Jerry studied her, she straightened her shoulders and made herself smile at him. It would hurt to leave her job but being near Jason, knowing how badly she had wounded him and knowing that she had lost her chance to have his love, hurt plenty more.

"I'm fine, Jerry. Really. It's a personal thing and I shouldn't let it affect my job the way I am. Next week I'll be better. I promise."

"Okay." He still didn't look convinced but after another awkward pat to her arm, he left her office.

———

"C'MON, LUCE. JOIN US FOR A QUICK DRINK. IT'S FRIDAY and you look like you've had one hell of a week. The way Jason's been treating you all week, you could use a drink," Carlos said.

"Thanks Carlos, but I'm really tired. I think I'll head home."

"Almost everyone's going. Have one quick drink - I'll buy - and then you can head home. You know you want to, Lucy-Lou," Carlos wheedled.

Lucy hesitated. She really didn't want to go home to her empty apartment and stare at all the spots that she and Jason had made love. It was unbelievably painful, and she was seriously considering moving just to get away from the memories of that brief weekend.

Carlos was still staring at her and she smiled suddenly at him. "You know what? You're right – I could use a drink. Count me in."

"That's great!" Carlos grinned delightedly at her before

glancing at his watch. "We're going to head out in about half an hour or so. I'll even give you a lift so if you have a bit too much to drink, I'll make sure you get home safe."

"Oh no, that won't be necessary," Lucy said.

Carlos winked at her. "You never know. Crazier things have happened at our Friday night get-togethers, Lucy Lou. In fact -"

"Ms. Reid!" Jason stood in the doorway of the lunchroom, glaring at both her and Carlos.

"Yes, Mr. Young?" She forced herself to look directly into his angry gaze.

"Have you finished reviewing the document I emailed to you?"

She frowned. "The one that's due on Tuesday?"

"I want it before you leave tonight."

"But you said in the email you wouldn't need it until Tuesday."

"And now I need it tonight," he said icily. "Is that a problem?"

"No. I'll have it on your desk before tomorrow," Lucy said.

He nodded, his nostrils flaring angrily, and left the lunchroom.

"Jesus, what an asshole," Carlos muttered.

"He isn't. I think he's under a lot of pressure right now," Lucy said.

"Stop defending him, Lucy. He's a complete dick to you and you know it," Carlos replied.

"Hush, Carlos. He's our boss and it will reflect badly on you if someone hears you talking that way. Anyway, I'd better get back to my office. I have a thirty-page document to review before tomorrow. Thanks for the invite. I'll catch you at the next one, okay?"

"Why don't you come for one drink and then come back to the office?" Carlos said.

"I'd better not. Have a good weekend. I'll see you Monday." Lucy waved and headed back to her office.

SATURDAY MORNING, JASON STUCK HIS HEAD INTO JERRY'S office. It was empty and he frowned before making his way to his own office. He'd received a weird text from Jerry asking him to meet him at the office immediately. He sat down at his desk and checked his email. Lucy had emailed him the document at eleven thirty last night. He sighed. He didn't need the document until Tuesday but standing outside the lunchroom, listening to Carlos inviting her for drinks and her accepting, had filled him with jealousy. He hadn't thought, just reacted, and forced her to stay at the office for hours to finish the document so she couldn't go out with the others.

Jerry walked into his office, dressed casually in jeans and a t-shirt. "Thanks for meeting me, Jason. We had a problem at the office last night. One of our employees was attacked as she was leaving the office."

"What?" Jason stared at Jerry in shock.

Jerry nodded and sank into the chair across from his desk. "We'll need to speak with the police and -"

"Who was it, Jerry?" Jason's stomach was in knots.

"Lucy."

"Oh my God." Panic rose in his throat. "Is she okay? How badly is she hurt? Where is she?"

"She's at the hospital. She was working late last night, and she was attacked in the parking garage as she walked to her car. Some homeless guy tried to mug her. She fought

43

back, and I guess the security guard heard her screaming." Jerry rubbed his forehead. "From now on, any of our female employees working late do not leave the office without the security guard escorting them."

"How badly is she hurt?" Jason asked hoarsely. He thought he might throw up. It was his fault that Lucy was attacked, and he would never forgive himself.

"She's got some bruised ribs, one hell of a black eye, and some bruising on her face. She had the hospital call her friend Amanda but when they couldn't get a hold of her, Lucy gave them Heather's cell phone number. With her parents living so far away, I think we're the closest people to family that she has here. We went to the hospital to pick her up, but they decided to keep her over night so they could do x-rays on her ribs and monitor her for a concussion. Heather is leaving in about half an hour to pick her up."

Jason stood and headed for the door.

"Jason, where are you going?"

"To the hospital."

Jerry followed him down the hall. "She's fine, Jason. Heather will pick her up and take her home. Or she can come back to our house if she doesn't want to be alone. I'll call you if -"

"I'll take her home and stay with her. I'll call you if we need anything." He didn't wait for Jerry's reply, just turned on his heel and practically ran out of the building.

"Lucy?"

Jason winced when Lucy turned her head to stare at him. Her right eye was puffy and bruised, and her bottom lip was split. There was a bruise along the line of her jaw, and she looked tired and pale.

"Hello, Mr. Young."

He sat down on the bed beside her. "How are you feeling?"

"Actually, I'm feeling pretty good. I didn't about half an hour ago. In fact, I felt like shit half an hour ago. Then the nurse came in and she put something in my IV, and now I have the most loveliest floaty feeling in the whole wide world." She smiled at him.

"I'm so sorry, little Lucy." He picked up her hand and held it tight.

She stared at him in genuine surprise. "Why? You didn't beat me up. I mean the whole thing is a little fuzzy, but I'm pretty sure it was a very smelly man with a truly awful plaid shirt who beat me up."

She giggled and squeezed his hand. "I suppose homeless people don't always have the best variety for clothing, but that shirt was an insult on the eyes. It really was. Hey, did I mention how good I feel right now?"

"You did." He smiled at her.

"The police took my statement last night. They said they would look for him, but they doubted they'd find him. They said he probably hopped on a bus and went bye-bye after the security guard scared him off." She released his hand and made a flying motion with her hands and then giggled again.

She sighed and closed her eyes. He held her hand again watching her face intently. He thought she might have dozed off when her eyes suddenly popped open. "Did you get the document I sent you?"

"I did, honey."

"Good, I'm glad. I haven't been very good at my job this week. I'm sorry." She stared solemnly at him.

"You've been fine. I'm sorry I made you stay late last night."

"Meh, it was no big deal. I got to practice my karate skills." She grinned at him, and then winced before touching the split in her lip. "He punched me in the face a few times, but I'm pretty sure I got in a kick to his balls."

"Honey," Jason said, "I'm so sorry. I shouldn't have -"

The door to her room opened and a man dressed in scrubs entered the room. "Good morning, Ms. Reid. How are you feeling?"

"Great!" Lucy said. "I feel really, really great."

The doctor scanned her chart that was hanging from the end of the bed. "I see you've received your pain meds this morning."

"Sure did. They're great. Really, really great." Lucy yawned and her eyes slipped closed again.

"Does she have any broken ribs?" Jason asked the doctor anxiously.

The doctor stared at him. "And you are?"

"I'm her boyfriend," Jason lied easily as he held his hand out. The doctor shook it and then glanced at Lucy's chart again.

"No, her ribs aren't broken, and she doesn't have a concussion. It's mostly scrapes and bruises. She got lucky. Her side is going to be pretty sore for about a week or so. She'll need to limit her movements and get some bed rest, but she should be feeling much better by this time next week."

He pulled a prescription pad from his pocket and wrote on it before tearing off the sheet of paper and handing it to Jason. "This is a prescription for some oral pain meds. Make sure she takes them with something to eat, every eight hours starting this afternoon. I'll discharge her now, but she shouldn't be alone."

"She's coming back to my house," Jason said. "I'll make sure she gets some rest and takes her medication."

"Good. Expect some bruising and tenderness around her ribs but if it isn't feeling a little better in a few days, bring her back to the hospital. We'll do more x-rays."

He walked to the bed and shook Lucy's shoulder lightly. "Ms. Reid?"

"What's up, Doc?" Lucy opened her eyes and blinked at him.

"I'm going to discharge you now. Your boyfriend is going to take you home and I've already told him you need to be on strict bed rest for a couple of days."

"So, I shouldn't practice my gymnastic routine. Is that what you're saying?" Lucy asked.

The doctor laughed. "That's exactly what I'm saying." He pulled the sheet down to the end of the bed.

"Fine, but when I don't make the Olympics, I'm sending my coach your way. He's Russian and kind of mean," Lucy warned.

The doctor laughed again. "I'll be on the lookout for him. I'm going to have the nurse take your IV out and then you can head home but first, I want to take one more look at your ribs."

"Okey dokey." Lucy reached out and snagged Jason's hand as the doctor lifted her hospital gown to just below her breasts. Jason sucked in his breath. Her right side was swollen, and the telltale signs of deep bruising had already risen on her skin. Her pale skin was covered in dark purple splotches, and Lucy watched with interest as the doctor probed gently at her side.

She winced and squeezed Jason's hand when the doctor probed a little lower. "Ouch!"

"Sorry," the doctor said. He examined the large bruise on

her left thigh. Rage rose in Jason when he realized the bruise was in the shape of a boot print.

"He kicked me after I fell down," Lucy said matter-of-factly.

The doctor examined her face last, pushing gently on the bruising around her eye, shining a small pen light into her pupils and feeling both sides of her jaw.

"You're very lucky that he didn't break anything," he said. "In fact, based on the bruising, I can't believe he didn't break or at least crack a rib."

Lucy rubbed her round tummy. "It's the extra layer of padding. It not only keeps me warm in the winter but also protects me from attempted muggings. The next time someone gives me a dirty look for eating a second cheese-burger, I'm gonna tell them it's a defense mechanism against random muggings."

The doctor burst out laughing before pulling her hospital gown down. "Take care, Ms. Reid. Don't hesitate to come back if you're feeling worse or the swelling doesn't go down after a few days."

"THIS ISN'T HEATHER AND JERRY'S HOUSE." LUCY HAD dozed off in the truck and it wasn't until he had her standing in the front hallway of his house that she realized where she was.

"I thought I was supposed to go to Jerry's. Heather said I could stay with them for a few days." She allowed Jason to pull off her shoes, holding onto his back for support as she lifted one foot and then the other.

"I told them I would take you to my house instead." He straightened and eased off her jacket.

"That's nice. You're so nice." She patted his cheek, and he took her hand and led her to his bedroom.

As he undressed her down to her panties she stared dreamily at his bed. "There's your bed. I've missed your bed."

She reached out and brushed her hand across it. "Hello, bed."

The cat jumped up on to the bed and she gave a soft squeak of delight. "There's your cat. I've missed your cat. Hello, Lenny."

She reached to pet him, and the cat bumped his head under her fingers, purring loudly.

"Lenny likes me," she announced.

"He does," Jason agreed. "C'mon, honey. Let's get you into bed."

"Yes, lets." She traced her hand down his chest before cupping his penis. "There's your cock. I've missed your cock. Hello, Jason's cock."

Despite his guilt and his worry for her, he couldn't help laughing. "Not for that, little Lucy. You need rest."

She snorted, swaying a little. "I'm fine. It'll take more than a mugging from a man in a really awful shirt to stop me. Hey, did I tell you how awful his shirt was?"

"You did, honey." Jason pulled back the covers and she climbed gingerly into the bed, flinching a little and holding onto her side.

"It was really, really bad." She stared up at him. "Promise me you'll never wear plaid, Jason."

"Okay."

"Say it – say I promise I'll never wear plaid, Lucy."

"I promise I'll never wear plaid, Lucy."

"Thank God." She blew her breath out in a soft little rush as he sat down on the bed beside her.

"Are you hungry, honey?"

She shrugged. "Maybe. I could probably eat some waffles."

"How about I make you some soup instead?"

"Sure."

He stood and she grabbed his hand. "Don't leave me!"

"I won't, honey."

She cocked her head at him, her dark eyes were rimmed with red and tired looking. "Say I promise I'll never leave you, Lucy."

"I promise I'll never leave you, Lucy."

"Good." Her eyes slipped closed. He stood where he was for a moment, wondering if he should try and get her to eat something or let her sleep.

Still purring, Lenny curled up against her hip and she opened her eyes and smiled. "Lenny likes me."

"I know. Do you want that soup?"

She shook her head. "No. I'm tired."

"I'll let you get some sleep. I'll be in the living room if you need me, okay?"

"Please stay with me," she pleaded. "I don't want to be alone. Will you stay?"

"Of course." He stripped off his clothes and slipped into the bed beside her. She turned carefully to her left side and curled into his body, putting her arm around his waist and burrowing her face into the curve of his neck.

He rested his hand on her hip and kissed the top of her shoulder. God, he missed her. Her rejection had nearly torn him apart, but it had done nothing to stop his love for her. Not that she would believe that. He'd treated her so horribly this week. He'd been furious with her and taken his pain out on her.

"I'm sorry I was so awful to you this week," he said. It was a lame apology, but he didn't know what else to say.

She shrugged. "It's fine. I upset you and made you sad."

She was quiet for a while and he shifted a little closer to her. She tipped her head back and squinted at him. "Jason?"

"Yeah?"

"Are you still in love with me?"

"Yeah, I am."

A look of relief crossed her face, and she dropped a soft kiss on his bare chest. "That's so nice. You're so nice."

She squinted up at him again. "Should I tell you a secret, Jason?"

"Yes, tell me."

"I'm in love with you. I lied before because I was scared, and because I didn't understand how I could fall in love with you so quickly," she said.

His heart began a crazy, jumbled beat in his chest as she looked at him solemnly. "Promise you won't tell anyone."

"I won't." His voice was suddenly raspy.

"Say it – say I promise I won't tell anyone you're in love with me, Lucy."

"I promise I won't tell anyone you're in love with me, Lucy," he repeated obediently. He couldn't stop the huge smile from crossing his face, and he could barely hear her whispered reply over the roar of his pulse in his ears.

"Good. I love you, Jason."

"I love you too, Lucy." He pulled her closer as her head dropped to his chest with a heavy thud and she slipped into sleep.

CHAPTER 5

Lucy laid perfectly still. She could hear the faint sound of the ocean and she frowned. Why could she hear the ocean from her apartment? And why did her body hurt so much?

She moved her arms experimentally. It brought a shooting pain through her side and she groaned. A truck started rumbling right next to her ear, and she opened her eyes and squinted in the late afternoon sun. Yellow eyes were staring into hers and the truck suddenly got louder.

"Lenny?" she whispered. The cat meowed and bumped his head against her face as his purring reached a level of sound roughly as loud as a bomb. She grunted with pain and pushed him away as everything that had happened came flooding back in a hot rush.

Shit.

She was in Jason's house. He had picked her up from the hospital and brought her back here, and while under the influence of some incredibly awesome pain relief medication she had told him that she loved him.

Double shit.

She stared at Jason's sleeping form. Dammit, she did love him. There was no point in denying it. She sighed and, moving slowly, sat up and swung her legs over the edge of the bed. She took careful stock of herself. Her eye hurt as did her thigh, she examined the boot mark briefly, but it was her side that hurt the most. She looked down at her ribs, sucking in her breath at the dark bruising. It was even worse now than it was this morning.

She stared out the window of Jason's bedroom as Lenny purred and rubbed against her bare back. She felt grimy and gross and wanted a shower. She slid off the bed and limped out of Jason's room and down to the bathroom.

She took a long, hot shower, using Jason's shampoo to wash her hair and his soap to gingerly wash her bruised body. The hot water helped ease both her stiffness and aching. By the time she had wrapped herself in a towel and stepped out of the tub, she was starting to feel almost human again.

She swiped the steam off the mirror and stared horrified at her reflection. Her eye was horribly swollen, and it was bloodshot and bruised. There was a deep split in her bottom lip, and the right side of her jaw was puffy and dark with bruising.

"Ugh," she said.

The door to the bathroom opened and Jason, wearing just his jeans, stared at her anxiously. "Are you okay?"

She nodded and turned her face away, tugging at the towel around her body. "Yeah."

He stepped into the small room and turned her face toward his. "You should eat something and take some more medication. Are you in pain?"

"Yeah, a little. It's mostly my side that hurts."

He pulled a t-shirt from a hook on the back of the door and helped her into it before leading her into the living room.

He wrapped her in a blanket and made her sit on the couch as he heated up soup for her.

He brought the steaming bowl of soup to her and said apologetically, "It's just from a can."

"It's fine. It smells good." She wasn't lying but the pain in her side was starting to be so bad that she felt sick to her stomach. She wasn't sure she could eat anything.

"Lucy? You're very pale." Jason knelt beside her. Her hand shaking, she spooned some soup into her mouth.

"I'm okay." She ate a few spoonsful of soup before pushing it away.

He frowned. "You need to eat more, honey."

"I'm full," she said.

He handed her a glass of water and two white pills. "Here, take these. It will help with the pain."

She swallowed the pills and then sat back on the couch, flinching at the stab of pain in her ribs.

"Do you remember what happened, Lucy?" Jason asked.

"Yeah. I do," she saod.

"I'm so sorry, honey. It's my fault. If I hadn't made you stay late -"

"Stop, Jason. It wasn't your fault. You needed the document."

"I didn't," he said. "I just couldn't stand the thought of you going to the bar with Carlos. I used the document as a reason to make you stay and then you were – were attacked. I'm so sorry."

He looked so miserable and upset that her heart ached for him. She reached out and cupped his face. "It's okay. Really. How could you have known what would happen?"

He placed a soft kiss in the palm of her hand before squeezing it. "Do you remember what happened after I brought you home from the hospital?"

She paused. She was tempted to lie and say that she couldn't remember but she couldn't bring herself to do that to him. "Yes, I remember."

He didn't reply and she gave a nervous laugh. "The things people will say while they're under the influence of drugs, huh?"

A look of hurt crossed his face but he masked it quickly and smiled at her. "Yeah, I figured it was the pills talking."

He went to stand up and she grabbed his hand. "Jason, wait. It wasn't just the pills talking. I do love you."

He released his breath in a harsh rush. "Really?"

"Yes, really." She scowled at him. "I love you – dammit."

He laughed. "Can I just say I'm really enjoying this romantic side of you, Lucy?"

"Shut it, you," she said. "We've both gone completely crazy. You know that, right?"

"I know I'm crazy about you."

"I'm not ready for other people to know about this. Do you understand?" she said.

He nodded. "I do. We can keep it quiet. I'm a private person anyway."

She sighed with relief and then rubbed her side again. "Thank you."

He stood and helped her to her feet. "You need some more rest."

He led her back to his bedroom and helped her into the bed. The meds were starting to kick in. The pain in her side was diminishing and her eyelids were growing heavy.

"Stay with me," she said.

"Always," he said and joined her in the bed.

Wrapped in a blanket and sitting on the futon on the deck, Lucy watched as Jason waded out of the water with his surfboard under one muscular arm. He was dressed in a full-body wetsuit, but she was still shocked when he told her he was going surfing. He joined her on the deck, stripping off his wetsuit and dressing in track pants and a t-shirt before dropping onto the futon beside her.

"Aren't you freezing?" she asked. It was early September and the days had turned cool. She could only imagine how cold the water was.

He laughed and shook his head so that she was sprinkled with water from his hair. "It's refreshing."

She wiped the cold drops of water off her face. "You're insane."

"Certifiably," he agreed.

He examined her face. It had been a week since he brought her home from the hospital. The split in her lip had healed but there was still fading yellow bruising around her eye. Her side was a colourful mess of greens, yellows, and purples, but the colour was back in her face and she had stopped taking the medication for pain.

She turned her head. "Ugh – don't look at me that closely. My face still looks like roadkill."

"Your face looks beautiful." He turned her face back to his and kissed her mouth. "Are you going back to work on Monday?"

"Yes."

"Are you sure you should go back this quickly?"

She laughed and gave him a sarcastic salute. "Yes, sir. I'm feeling much better."

He growled playfully at her. "Don't make me spank you for impudence."

Her breath caught in her throat as a slow pulse of pleasure

moved from her stomach and straight to her crotch. She'd been at Jason's house for the entire week. He had taken her home to grab clothes and toiletries and she hadn't even considered staying there. She wanted to be with him - needed to be with him - and they hadn't even discussed it. He simply found her suitcase in the closet and helped her pack her things.

She slept each night in his bed and wrapped in his arms, but the pain had tampered her desire. Today, feeling normal and pain-free for the first time since the mugging, she was very aware of Jason's warmth and hard body.

"Who called earlier?" she asked.

"Jerry. He wondered how you were doing, and if you were coming back to work on Monday. I told him I thought you were but that I would call him if you needed more time."

"Did he – did he ask why I was still at your house?"

"Nope."

She didn't reply and he squeezed her knee through the blanket. "Are you hungry?"

"Yes." She was hungry but it wasn't for food.

"I can make you some waffles if you'd like."

She glanced to the house on the right. "Are your neighbours still on holidays?"

"Nah. They got back two weeks ago. I think they're gone for the weekend though. Their daughter is getting married." He squeezed her knee again. "I'll get started on the waffles."

"I'm not hungry for waffles," Lucy said before rubbing his upper thigh.

HIS WILLPOWER WAS MUSH AROUND HER. THE MOMENT LUCY told him she wasn't hungry for waffles and touched his leg,

58

his cock hardened in his pants. He was aching for her. A week of sleeping next to her warm body, of listening to her soft voice and watching her live in his house like she belonged there, kept him in a constant state of arousal.

Afraid of hurting her, he ignored his need even when it became obvious that she was healed. He wasn't just worried about hurting her physically. Despite her proclamation of love, things still felt fragile between them and he didn't want to do anything that would upset her.

She unwrapped the blanket and reclined on the futon, resting her head on the pillow before placing one foot on the floor of the deck and sliding the other behind his back. She was wearing one of his t-shirts and nothing else. He stared hungrily at the sight of her naked core as she crooked her finger at him. "Come here, handsome."

"Are you sure? I don't want to hurt you."

"You won't." She smiled again at him. "I'm freezing, Jason. Warm me up."

He covered her body with his own, resting on his knees between her open thighs so he didn't put any pressure on her ribs. He kissed her forehead. "We should go inside. It's too cold out here for you."

She kissed him before whispering against his lips, "No, I want you to take me out here. Make me feel good, Jason. Please."

He wrapped the blanket around the them until they were cocooned in its warmth and, balancing carefully on his knees and one hand, dipped his other hand between her legs. She was soaking wet already and he looked at her in surprise.

She grinned. "Watching you walk out of the ocean in that skin-tight wetsuit got me all hot and bothered."

He dipped his head and kissed her tenderly as she reached between them and tugged at the waistband of his track pants until his cock sprung free. She wrapped her hand around it. Her fingers were cold but her mouth and body were warm, and he swelled in her hand.

"Lucy," he moaned as she stroked his shaft with long, hard pulls. "I need to get a condom."

She wiggled her free hand out of the blanket and reached under the pillow. There was the crinkling of a wrapper and she showed him the condom.

"Do you just carry one of those around with you all the time now, Ms. Reid?" He arched his eyebrow at her, and she giggled.

"Only when I'm around you, Mr. Young."

She released him long enough to tear open the condom and slide it onto his throbbing erection. He moaned again. The feel of her fingers sliding on the condom was almost enough to make him come, and he thrust his hips hungrily against her as he kissed her.

"You make me so hot," she whispered. "I'm close to coming and you've barely touched me."

He groaned. "Quickly, little Lucy. I need you."

She guided his cock into her pussy, both sighing with pleasure as he slid easily into her slick warmth. He pushed in and out of her in a slow, deep rhythm as she moaned beneath him.

"That's so good, Jason. Right there, just like that," she breathed into his ear.

He could feel her hard nipples brushing against his chest even through their clothing, and he groaned and thrust a little harder into her.

"Oh yes," she moaned again. Her breath was quickening, and her face was flushed with pleasure as he plunged in and out of her.

"Faster now. Please, Jason," she pleaded.

"I don't want to hurt you," he panted.

"You won't." She squeezed his arms.

He increased the rhythm of his body within hers. She opened her eyes and gave him a smile of such sweetness that he could feel an almost painful surge of love for her rush through his body.

"I love you, Lucy," he gasped out as she arched her hips upward to meet his quick rhythm.

"I love you too, Jason."

"Again. Say it again," he muttered.

"I love you. I love you. I love you." She suddenly stiffened under him, her eyes closing as the late afternoon light danced across her face and her body shook with her orgasm.

He could feel his body shuddering, feel the heat growing in his belly as he headed toward his own release. He tried to hold back. He tried to delay the pleasure for as long as possible but when she kissed his neck and whispered that she loved him, he climaxed hard inside of her.

CHAPTER 6

*A*re you going tonight?

Lucy read the text from Jason and smiled a little.

Yes, and I think you should go too. A boss should socialize with the staff occasionally. Maybe buy them a round of drinks.

He didn't reply, and she tucked her phone away and returned to studying the document in front of her. She knew he would be at the bar tonight. He'd gone to the last two Friday night get-together's because she went. She doubted he enjoyed it. Although most of the single women in the office had given up on their efforts to seduce him, Alex and June were still adamant they were going to win the bet. The previous Friday night he was sandwiched between the two of them, shooting pointed looks at her while she tried not to smile.

It had been a month since the hospital. She spent nearly every night at his house. The two or three nights that she left work and went to her apartment instead, Jason showed up a few hours later and stayed the night at her place. They couldn't seem to get enough of each other.

63

She stared blankly at the document on her desk. They were careful - very careful - at work and she was positive that no one suspected. Jason wasn't rude to her any longer, but he was almost prudently polite and professional with her.

She traced her finger along the words on the document. Well, almost no one at work suspected. Although he hadn't said a word to either of them, she was sure Jerry knew something was going on between her and Jason. Even if Heather hadn't told him, the fact that Jason took her home after the hospital and she stayed at his house must have tipped him off.

She sighed and forced herself to concentrate on her work. It didn't matter. She hadn't told Jason, but she'd been scanning the employment ads for the last two weeks, looking for a new job. She loved working here, but she loved Jason more, and she was tired of keeping their relationship a secret. A new job was a small price to pay to not have to hide her feelings for him.

"CAN YOU BELIEVE BOTH JERRY AND JASON CAME TONIGHT?" Penny shouted into her ear.

Lucy shrugged. "I guess they were both feeling particularly social tonight."

"I guess. It's cool and everything but I sort of feel like we need to be on our best behaviour. We don't want our bosses seeing us drunk and dancing on the tables." Penny grinned at her.

Lucy laughed. "Since when have I ever joined you in dancing on the tables?"

Penny giggled. "It'll happen one day." She glanced across the table where Carlos was taking a sip of beer. "So, are you going to hit that or what?"

"Penny!"

"What? He is obviously in to you. Just wondering when you're going to finally take him home."

"I'm not," Lucy said. Her gaze cut to Jason who was sitting a few chairs down from them, talking with Jerry. As usual, Alex was seated next to him, but she was looking decidedly dejected.

It was mean but Lucy couldn't help smiling a little. Jason had spent the entire night chatting with Jerry and with Paul sitting across from him, and it looked like Alex was finally starting to get the hint.

She watched as Jason pulled his cell phone from his pocket and, with an apologetic look to Jerry, answered it. He stood and strolled across the noisy bar before slipping out the front door. She followed him with her gaze, twitching when Penny poked her.

"That man fills out a pair of jeans better than any other man we know, am I right?"

"I hadn't noticed."

"Bullshit," Penny said amiably. "Everyone notices Jason's ass. Hell, even Carlos notices it."

At the sound of his name, Carlos leaned forward. "What was that?"

"Nothing," Penny said sweetly. "Just talking about how great your ass looks tonight, Carlos."

He blushed and both Lucy and Penny grinned.

"Well then, pretty Penny. I think that comment deserves a beer. Your next one is on me," he drawled.

She giggled. "You're such a gentleman, Carlos."

She stood and tugged Lucy with her. "We're going to go and freshen up. Excuse us."

Lucy followed her to the ladies' room. They stood in front

of the mirror and Lucy watched Penny smooth her hair and reapply her lipstick.

"So, listen," Penny said. "if you're not interested in Carlos, I was thinking I might - you know – become a little friendlier with him. If you're okay with it?"

Lucy grinned. "I'm perfectly fine with it. I hope it -"

She cried out at the sudden loud explosion from within the bar. The floor swayed beneath their feet, and she grabbed onto Penny as the fire alarm went off with a whooping bray. The water sprinklers sprayed on, immediately soaking them, and Penny stared at her with large, frightened eyes.

"Lucy? What's happening?"

"I don't know. C'mon, we need to get out of here," Lucy said.

She pulled Penny to the door and pushed it open. Immediately, a huge cloud of black smoke rolled in and they were blinded. They could feel the heat and hear the crackling of the flames. Coughing and gagging, the two women stepped back and let the door shut.

Penny fanned the smoke from her face as more seeped under the door. The small bathroom was rapidly filling with smoke, and Penny grabbed onto her with panicky tightness. Her blonde hair was soaking wet from the sprinklers and more water was beading down her face.

"Lucy! What's happening? What do we do?"

"We need to get out of here." Lucy swallowed down her own panic. She was terrified for herself and for Penny, but she was also filled with terror for Jason. Please God, she prayed silently. Let him still be outside.

She coughed again, the smoke searing her throat, and stared around the room. "There! The window – let's go!"

She pushed the smaller woman toward the window set

high in the wall at the far end of the bathroom. Penny stumbled to it and reached upwards.

"I can't reach it, Lucy!" she cried. She stared at the door of the bathroom as muffled screams of panic and fear could be heard.

There was a large round garbage can under the sink and Lucy grabbed it. She tipped it over, spilling paper towels across the floor. She dragged it under the window, slipping and sliding on the wet floor. She climbed on top of it and opened the latch on the window. It was a push window and it opened only halfway before stopping.

"Fuck!"

Penny stared up at her in terror. "We're trapped!"

"No, we're not."

Lucy shut the window and yanked off her jacket. She wrapped it around her arm and fist and turned her face away. She could barely see Penny through the smoke that had filled the bathroom.

"Penny, turn away. Cover your face!" she shouted before coughing and gagging on the smoke-filled air.

Penny turned away obediently and, shielding her own face with her other arm, Lucy hit the glass of the window. It cracked but didn't break and she screeched with frustration and fear before pounding on it again. This time the window shattered, and she cried out with relief as a cold night air drifted in. She peered through the window and could have sobbed with relief when she saw that it was only about a ten-foot drop to the alleyway.

She quickly pushed all of the shards of glass out of the frame, and then placed her jacket on the bottom edge of the window frame to help protect them further. She held her hand down to Penny. "Climb up, quickly!"

Penny climbed up and the women clung to each other, balancing carefully on the overturned garbage can.

"I'm going to help you through the window. If you hang onto the window frame and lower yourself down, it'll only be about a five-foot drop for you," Lucy said. "Watch the glass, okay?"

She put her hand on Penny's butt and shoved her up and through the window. Penny straddled the ledge and, with one final panicked look at Lucy, eased both legs out and hung down from the ledge. She looked below her and moaned. "Lucy, I – I can't."

"Yes, you can!" Lucy coughed and squeezed the top of Penny's hands. "It's not that far, Penny. Just let go, honey."

With a frightened squeak, Penny let go and dropped to the ground. She hit the alleyway with a thud and rolled over onto her back.

"Penny! Are you okay?"

She sat up. "Yeah, I'm okay. Hurry, Lucy." She staggered to her feet and stared anxiously at Lucy.

Resting her hands on the bottom ledge, Lucy boosted herself up to the window. Panting and grunting with effort she pushed her leg out the window. She seized the side of the window frame and winced as some stray glass dug into the palm of her hand. She gritted her teeth and ignored it, pulling herself into a straddling position on the window.

Another explosion rocked the building and she nearly tumbled head-first out the window.

"Lucy!" Penny screamed in terror.

Her heart beating fiercely, Lucy squirmed out of the window. She balanced on her stomach on the coat-covered ledge, her top half in the bathroom and her bottom half dangling down the cold brick wall.

She took a deep breath, lowered herself out the window until she was dangling by her hands, and let go.

"JERRY! JERRY!"

Jerry, his bald head covered in soot and his shirt and jeans clinging wetly to him, stared blankly at Jason.

"Jerry! Where's Lucy? Where's Lucy?" Jason shook the older man so hard he heard his teeth snap.

"I – I don't know," Jerry said. "She wasn't at the table when – when it happened."

He touched some blood that was oozing out of the top of his skull and stared dully at it. "There was a loud bang, and the kitchen door blew off its hinges. I think – I think something exploded in there. There was so much smoke, and then fire came billowing out of the kitchen."

Jerry gave him another dazed look. "People were screaming and fighting to get to the door."

Jason stared around him. There were small clusters of people from the bar standing in the parking lot, and they were staring at the burning building with shell-shocked gazes. With the exception of Penny and Lucy, the people from the office were gathered in a loose group next to Jerry. He pushed past Jerry and grabbed Carlos' arm. The smaller man stared at him numbly.

"Where's Lucy? Carlos!" He shook him impatiently. "Where's Lucy? Have you seen her? Was she with you?"

Carlos shook his head. "No. She – she and Penny went to the bathroom right before the fire. I think they're still in there."

"Oh my God," Jason whispered. He turned and ran for the burning building as sirens filled the cold night air.

"Jason! Stop!" Jerry shouted after him.

Jason ignored him. He had to get in there. He had to find Lucy. If she died…

Adrenaline was coursing through his veins, sending his heartbeat into jittery, rapid overdrive. He couldn't live without her. He couldn't –

"Jason!"

He skidded to a stop. Lucy, followed by Penny, was limping out of the alleyway to the left of the burning bar. Her jacket was missing, and she was soaking wet and covered in soot. Even from here he could see blood dripping from her right hand, but she was alive.

He screamed her name and she limped faster. He sprinted across the parking lot. She was crying and shaking, and she stumbled as she hobbled toward him. He caught her before she could fall and crushed her against his body. "Lucy!"

She hugged him, burying her face in his neck as hot tears dripped down her face. "You're okay."

He eased her back and covered her face with kisses before pressing his mouth hard against hers. She returned his kiss, balancing on one foot and squashing her wet body against his. He released her mouth and stared down at her. "Are you all right, honey?"

She nodded. "Yeah. I cut my hand on some glass, and I twisted my ankle when I dropped out of the bathroom window, but I'll live."

She smiled at him and he kissed her again before hugging her hard.

"Lucy?" Penny's voice cut through the sirens that were growing steadily louder. She was staring at them with shock. "You and – and Jason?"

Lucy opened her mouth, but nothing came out. She looked to her left. A small moan of dismay squeaked out of her throat when she realized that the entire group from the office was staring at them.

Jason picked her up and cradled her against his chest before starting across the parking lot, Penny trailing after them.

"Jason…"

She gave him a look of panic and he shook his head.

"It doesn't matter, little Lucy. I thought – I thought I had lost you. You're alive and that's all that matters, not what anyone thinks of us. Do you understand?"

"Yes. I love you, Jason."

"I love you too, Lucy."

"HOW'S YOUR ANKLE?" JASON SHIFTED THE ICE PACK ON HER foot before sitting on the bed beside her.

"It's fine." She smiled reassuringly at him and stroked his face. "Stop worrying."

Lenny jumped onto the bed and head butted her arm. She petted his head, wincing when he kneaded her thigh with his sharp claws.

"Go on, Lenny." Jason frowned and pushed lightly at the cat.

"I don't mind." She took his hand and squeezed it.

He stared at her in silence for a moment and then said, "Move in with me, Lucy."

"What?" She blinked at him.

"Move in with me. I love you and Lenny loves you."

She smiled and he hurried on. "You practically live here anyway. Why pay rent on an apartment that you're never in? I want to go to bed every night next to you, and I want to wake up every morning with you beside me."

"Jason -"

"The place is small I know. Too small probably, but we can buy a larger place. It doesn't even have to be on the beach. I don't care, I -"

"Jason, stop," she said. "I love this place and I love Lenny, and I love you. Of course I'll move in with you."

He smiled with relief. "Good. We'll start moving your things in tomorrow."

She laughed. "Maybe we'll let my ankle heal first. What do you say?"

"Right, your ankle." He shifted the ice pack again and she reached out and cupped his face, turning it toward her. She kissed him, brushing her tongue across his lips until he opened his mouth.

She took his hand and pressed it to her breast, and he groaned into her mouth. "We can't, little Lucy. Your ankle."

"I don't need my ankle for what I'm going to do to you," she said with a grin.

She reclined on the pillows and pulled him on top of her. As he trailed a path of blazing hot kisses down her neck, she stared up at the ceiling. Her fear about being caught by the others, her worry about what they would think of her and Jason, had disappeared. She knew what she had to do, and first thing Monday morning she would speak to Jerry. Her job didn't matter. What mattered was how she felt about Jason.

JASON KNOCKED ON JERRY'S OFFICE DOOR. AT HIS ANSWER, he opened it and sat down in the leather chair across from the desk.

It was Monday morning. Lucy had slipped out early, waking him up with a soft kiss and a whispered goodbye. She must have had a deadline for Jerry. Normally they left at the same time, kissing goodbye before leaving for the office in their separate vehicles.

"Good morning, Jason." Jerry sat back in his chair and crossed his arms over his trim stomach. "How was the rest of your weekend? I'm assuming a lot quieter than Friday night?"

"Yeah." Jason nodded. "How's everyone else?"

"They seem okay. I'm going to call a meeting in an hour or so with everyone who was there. I want to see how they're doing. Everyone showed up for work this morning – I consider that a good sign."

"It is." Jason cleared his throat. "Listen, Jerry, I'm here because I wanted you to know that I'm resigning. I love Lucy. We've been hiding our relationship because Lucy didn't want the others to know."

"They know now. Why quit?" Jerry asked.

Jason shrugged. "I think it would be easier for Lucy if I didn't work here. She loves her job, and she doesn't want you or the others treating her differently because we're dating."

"I'm not accepting your resignation, Jason."

Jason gave him a dry look. "You're not the one I give my resignation to, Jerry."

Jerry shrugged. "Yeah, I know. I didn't accept Lucy's resignation when she hobbled into my office first thing this morning, and I'll talk the Board of Directors into not accepting yours."

"Lucy tried to quit?"

"Yes. I'm going to tell you the same thing I told her. No one in the office cares if you're sleeping together. And if they do? That's their problem, not yours. Lucy was a damn hard worker before you came along, and she'll continue to be regardless of whether she's dating you or not."

"It's you she's worried about the most, Jerry. She doesn't want you to think differently about her."

Jerry studied him silently for a moment. "My very first management job was with a construction company. Did you know that?"

Jason shook his head and Jerry continued. "Two years after I was promoted to management, our receptionist retired, and HR hired a new one. I was away at a job site, so I didn't even get to meet the new candidate, let alone interview with her. I returned from the job site, walked into the office and there was this dark-haired goddess sitting at the front desk. She looked up and smiled and said, 'Good morning, you must be Mr. Hanson.' Her voice was musical and her eyes – they were a clear green that a man could get lost in."

Jerry stared at his desk. "I fell in love with her that very day. I fought my feelings for nearly a year, believing they were inappropriate and worried what others would think. Until one day we were both working late, and I just blurted them out."

He smiled at Jason. "I was lucky. She felt the same way. A year later I married her, and I've spent the last thirty-two years getting lost every day in those green eyes of hers. Trust me, Jason, I understand being attracted to a co-worker. Heather and I worked together for another five years until she went on maternity leave with our first."

He straightened and rested his hands on the desk. "I know you run the company but I'm second-in-command and Lucy's direct supervisor. I don't see a problem with the two of you dating, and I've already spoken with HR. We'll have you both sign letters stating that you won't let your personal relationship affect your job performance, and that will be the end of it. And neither of you are quitting. Do I make myself clear?"

Jason nodded, feeling a swell of gratitude toward the man. "You do."

"Good. I'll see you later at the meeting, okay?"

"Yes." Jason stood and walked towards the door. "Thank you, Jerry."

"You're welcome."

———

LUCY TURNED AT THE SOFT KNOCK, SMILING AT JASON. "Hi, you."

"Hi, yourself. How's the ankle?"

She looked down at her bandaged ankle. "It's good."

He continued to lean in her doorway. "I just finished speaking with Jerry. I told him I was quitting."

"Did he let you?"

He shook his head and she smiled. "Yeah, he wouldn't let me quit either."

"I heard."

"Did he tell you about him and Heather?"

"He did."

She nodded and looked at an envelope sitting on her desk for a moment before she glanced at him, her dark eyes soft and warm. "We'll make it work, won't we?"

"Yeah, Luce, we will."

Her hand smoothed across the envelope and he nodded towards it. "What's that?"

"This?" She held the envelope up with a little twinkle in her eye. "Alex dropped this off for me. All things considered she was pretty gracious about it."

She opened the envelope and turned it upside down. A piece of paper slid out and she held it up so he could read it.

A slow smile crossed his face. "Is that a gift certificate to 'Heaven's Gate Spa'?"

She winked at him. "It is. I'm wondering – do you have any plans for this weekend?"

"As a matter of fact, my weekend is totally open."

"Good. How'd you like to join me at the 'Heaven's Gate Spa'?"

"I'd love to, little Lucy."

Her grin widened. "I was hoping you'd say that."

He turned to go and paused in her doorway. "I'm making waffles for dinner. I'll see you at home, Ms. Reid?"

She smiled brilliantly at him. "I'll see you at home, Mr. Young."

Keep reading for an excerpt of the third novella in the Tempted Series, "Forever Tempted"

FOREVER TEMPTED EXCERPT

"Don't be nervous."

"I'm not nervous," Lucy said.

Jason arched his eyebrow at her, and she said, "I'm not nervous – I'm terrified."

He pulled her into his embrace. "You don't need to be. Technically you've already met my parents."

"Video chatting with them a couple of times is not the same as meeting them in person," Lucy said.

He kissed her forehead. "My parents are going to love you."

"Right," Lucy said before squirming out of his embrace. She studied herself in the mirror as Jason pulled on his jeans.

She thought she looked okay for a first parent meeting. Her thick, dark hair was somewhat contained by a clip and she had decided to go with just a bit of blush, a touch of mascara, and some soft pink gloss on her lips. Jason's parents were older, and she didn't want to meet them looking like the whore of Babylon.

Speaking of which – she turned to Jason. "Is my shirt too tight?"

He shook his head as he buckled his belt. "Personally, I don't think it's tight enough."

"Be serious," she said. "Do my boobs look huge?"

He grinned. "Baby, your boobs *are* huge."

"Gah," she muttered. "I really need to look into that reduction surgery."

The look of immediate horror on Jason's face was enough to make her forget her nerves. She laughed as he crossed the room and wrapped his arms around her waist.

"You didn't just say that. Tell me you didn't just say that."

She laughed again. "Careful, honey. Keep acting like that and I'll start to think you're only with me because of my breasts."

He cupped her breasts before kissing her neck. "They're only seventy-five percent of the reason I'm with you."

She whacked him lightly on the ass as he traced the shell of her ear with his tongue. When she spoke, her voice was breathless. "And the other twenty-five percent?"

"Your intelligence and your sweetness," he murmured. He ran his thumb over her nipple and she moaned.

"And the way you look handcuffed to the bed," he continued.

She snorted laughter before nipping his bottom lip. "I'm starting to seriously wonder if you're a sex addict."

He shook his head. "Nope, just a Lucy addict."

"Cheeseball."

He grinned and kissed her, slipping his tongue into her mouth to dart and lick and tease until her hips were pressing against his growing erection.

"I'm not a sex addict," he said before sliding his hand under her shirt.

"I've lived with you for nearly two months, and I can count on one hand the days we haven't had sex," Lucy said.

"We haven't had sex today," Jason said. "Something I fully intend to correct."

"We don't have time," she said as he cupped her breast.

"We have plenty of time." He sucked on the sensitive skin of her throat and she moaned before trying to push away from him.

"We really don't. Your parents' flight arrives in less than two hours and we still have to drive to the airport."

"I'll drive fast." His hands slid behind her back and unclipped her bra before she could even think to stop him.

"Jason," she moaned as he tugged her shirt over her head, stripped away her bra, and latched on to one throbbing nipple. He sucked hard at it as he pushed his hand between her legs and rubbed his thumb roughly against the denim that covered her warmth.

"Dammit, Jason," she muttered as she arched into his hand. "You don't play fair."

He grinned against her breast before pulling on her nipple with his teeth. She cried out and reached for his belt, fumbling the buckle open as he unbuttoned her jeans and shoved them and her panties down her legs.

"We have to be fast," she panted.

ABOUT THE AUTHOR

Elizabeth Kelly was born and raised in Ontario, Canada. She moved west as a teenager and now lives in Alberta with her husband and a menagerie of pets. She firmly believes that a person can survive solely on sushi and coffee, and only her husband's mad cooking skills prevents her from proving that theory.

For more information about Elizabeth, check out her website at

www.elizabethkelly.ca

facebook.com/EKellyBooks

twitter.com/ElizabethKBooks

instagram.com/elizabethkelly_author

amazon.com/Elizabeth-Kelly/e/B00EOHZ0MS

bookbub.com/authors/elizabeth-kelly

ALSO BY ELIZABETH KELLY

Tempted Series

Tempted

Twice Tempted

Forever Tempted

Breathless

Tempted Trilogy (Books 1-3)

Red Moon Series

Red Moon

Red Moon Rising

Dark Moon

Alpha Moon

Pale Moon

The Recruit Series

The Recruit (Book One)

The Recruit (Book Two)

The Recruit (Book Three)

The Recruit (Book Four)

The Recruit (Book Five)

The Shifters Series

Willow and the Wolf (Book One)

Ava and the Bear (Book Two)

Katarina and the Bird (Book Three)

Porter's Mate (Book Four)

Bria and the Tiger (Book Five)

Rosalie Undone (Book Six)

The Dragon's Mate (Book Seven)

Rise of the Jaguar (Book Eight)

The Draax Series

Reign (Book One)

Rule (Book Two)

Rebel (Book Three)

Harmony Falls Series

Sweet Harmony (Book One)

Perfect Harmony (Book Two)

Forbidden Harmony (Book Three)

Redeeming Harmony (Book Four)

Individual Books

The Necessary Engagement

Amelia's Touch

The Rancher's Daughter

Healing Gabriel

The Contract

A Home for Lily

Saving Charlotte

Shameless

The Fairy Tales Collection

Broken

An Unlikely Seduction

Holiday Romance

The Christmas Wife

The Christmas Rescue

The Christmas Nanny

The Christmas Boss

Sordid Games

www.ingramcontent.com/pod-product-compliance
Lightning Source LLC
Chambersburg PA
CBHW051925220626
47052CB00003B/586